Do Not Go Gentle

Published by Accent Press Ltd – 2014

ISBN 9781783755233

Copyright © Phil Carradice 2014

The Quick Reads project in Wales is an initiative coordinated by the Welsh Books Council and supported by the Welsh Government.

Printed and bound by CPI Group (UK) Ltd, Croydon, CR0 4YY

Cover design by Midnight Designs

CYNGOR LLYFRAU CYMRU
WELSH BOOKS COUNCIL

Noddir gan
Lywodraeth Cymru
Sponsored by
Welsh Government

Do Not Go Gentle

Phil Carradice

ACCENT PRESS LTD

Quick Reads 2014

Congratulations on choosing a 2014 Quick Read.

The Quick Reads project, with bite-sized books, is designed to get readers back into the swing of reading, and reading for pleasure. So we hope you enjoy this book.

What's your opinion?

Your feedback can make this project better. Once you've read one of the Quick Reads series, visit www.readingwales.org.uk or Twitter #quickreads2014 to post your feedback.

- Why did you choose this book?
- What did you like about it?
- What do you think of the Quick Reads series?
- Which Quick Reads would you like to see in the future?

What next?

Once you've finished one Quick Read – have you got time for another?

Look out for other titles in the 2014 Quick Reads series.

The room is coldly white, like hospital rooms the world over. White walls, white bed, white sheets. Even the nurses are dressed in white, in stiff, starched uniforms that creak when they walk or bend over the figure in the bed. Like giant seagulls they hover and swoop at the faintest sound.

Above the headboard of the bed, half hidden by the oxygen tent, is a white nameplate. 'Dylan Marlais Thomas, admitted 11/5/1953' – written the American way, with the month before the day. Not that anybody takes much notice. Such detail hardly matters to those who sit and wait.

He doesn't move, the figure in the bed, just lies there like a rock on the seashore. He breathes slowly, noisily, through his nose. The tubes and wires that snake away from his body to the side of the bed, and the oxygen tent, make him seem like some science fiction robot.

Visitors have come and gone all day but, apart from the nurse and the patient, at the moment there is just one person in the room. He is a bearded man of medium height. He waits and he watches, staring around the room as if he is waiting for somebody to jump out and attack him. Eventually he sighs. The nurse glances across at him.

"It is sad, isn't it?" she says. "A writer like him, a man of such wonderful words. And now there are no words, no words at all."

The bearded man nods. "I guess so," he says, his mid-west accent surprisingly strong. "But it'll come to us all, sooner or later. The one guarantee we've got in life is that we'll all leave it sometime."

The nurse stares at him, trying to work out if he is serious or trying to be funny with her. Finally she decides that his words are genuine.

"Are you a poet, too, Mr Berryman?"

The man smiles, embarrassed but happy to be included.

"A little poet. Not like him." He points to the patient and then they lapse into silence again. Only the heavy breathing of the man in the bed breaks the quiet of the hospital room. Berryman sighs again and yawns. He tries to hide the yawn behind his hand – waiting for someone to die, even if he is a great poet – is tiring.

"I'm going outside for a smoke," he says. "That's OK, isn't it?"

The nurse nods. "That's fine, Mr Berryman. He doesn't know if you're sitting there or not. He can't see or hear anything."

Of course I can bloody hear. I'm not dead. Not yet, at least. I've just gone back, retreated, you could say, to somewhere safe, somewhere nobody can hurt me. Nothing unusual in that, I've done it all my life. First sign of a cold or sniffle? Bed, with Mam feeding me milky bread and sugar. Caitlin, my Cat, used to do it too – feed me, comfort me. But that was when she still loved me.

It's restful, lying here like this. No more decisions to make, no problems to sort out, and the world such a long way away. It's not telling a lie – and, believe me, I know all about telling lies – when I say I'm happy to be here, happy for the first time since Dad died.

I've always told lies. Why tell the truth, I think, when a lie can be so much more interesting? Except that waiting here like this, it doesn't seem important to make things up any more. So maybe it's time for a little baring of the soul, a little telling of the truth. I'll try, anyway.

Childhood was magical. Not perfect, there were far too many rows and arguments for that – rows between Mam and Dad, between Nancy and me, between me and everyone really, apart from Mam – but still magical. Spoilt? You could say. Ruined to the point of cruelty, one very tidy uncle, a vicar and man of the church, used to

3

say. He also said I ought to be in a madhouse. He may have had a point.

It was warm, that house in Cwmdonkin Drive, always warm, no matter what the weather outside was up to. And as I remember it, the wind was always blowing in from the Bristol Channel, battering the slates off the roofs. I suppose that's what comes of building houses so high up on the side of the hill – they didn't name the area Uplands for nothing. Our house was Number 5. Number 5, Cwmdonkin Drive, in, what did I once call Swansea? That 'ugly, lovely town' by the sea.

It's a winter Sunday evening, Dad in his study, marking school exercise books, Mam making tea in the scullery. The scullery is where the cooking and washing-up takes place, the kitchen being the room where we eat and live most of the time. That leaves the other room downstairs for 'best' – very important in any Welsh home at that time.

My sister Nancy is upstairs, dressing herself ready to go out. And me, sitting under the guttering kitchen gaslight, reading something I have pulled from Dad's bookshelves. The wind blows and the rain beats, as it always does, against the windows of the house.

"Dylan! Have you been in my bag again?"

Nancy's voice echoes around the house. I hear Dad swear and slam shut the study door to keep out the noise of the argument. Me? Been in Nancy's bag? Of course I have. She's always worth the odd half a crown or ten bob.

"Not me," I shout as Nancy storms into the kitchen. "Mam, tell her."

"Leave the boy alone," Mam says, coming in from the scullery. "He wouldn't steal off you, Nancy dear."

I smile, sweetly – buckets of sick – at them both. Mam takes her purse and pulls out a ten-shilling note.

"Here, take this, dear," she says. "You probably just mislaid it. But take this anyway."

Nancy snatches the note. "That boy will end up in a reformatory," she snaps. "Or prison. You spoil him, mother." The door slams behind her and I go back to my book.

See what I mean about lies? I couldn't help myself back then and I can't help myself now. So although I'll try to be truthful, I'm not promising anything. Perhaps it's part of being a writer. You never know where the truth starts or ends, never know when your imagination is about to take over.

And stealing? Well, that came naturally, too. I've always said that my job is to write – poetry and stories, radio and film scripts – and not to worry about things like money or jobs. Let the ravens feed us, I've always thought, the soft, white silly ravens. By which I mean anyone out there who feels like helping. Or even those who don't.

Stealing was a part of childhood. We all did it but, to be honest with you, I was the best, had the quickest hands – and the strongest nerve. Mrs Ferguson's sweet shop in the Grove, at the bottom of our hill, was an Aladdin's cave to us.

"We're going to the pictures," Jim or Dan or Tom would say. "The Uplands Cinema. There's a new gangster film on. Get us some sweets, Dylan."

"What do you fancy?" I'd say.

The answer was always the same – "Wine gums."

We'd dive in through the door of her shop and ask for lemonade. The moment old Mrs Ferguson went into the back room to get it, my hands were into the box. Then later, pockets stuffed, I'd hand them out as the images of Charlie Chaplin, Rudolph Valentino or Buster Keaton flickered across the screen and we lay on

6

the broken seats at the back of the fleapit picture house.

Sometimes we would smoke cigarettes, even cigars if I could get them. Not that I ever bought any but you could file farthings – still around in those days – to use as sixpenny pieces in the cigarette machines. And I always had a good supply of farthings on hand. Oh, I was a bad boy.

Cwmdonkin Park, almost across the road from our house, was my playground. It was where I learned to run and hide, to let my imagination go wild. It was where I first became a pirate captain, a wagon train scout, an explorer in the Arctic or African wilderness. If you've ever read my poem 'The Hunchback in the Park' you'll have a pretty good idea of what it meant to me. As the old park-keeper in my radio broadcast *Return Journey* once said: "I remember him well. I think he was happy all the time."

Of course, I went further afield as well. The Mumbles and the Gower Peninsula were on our doorstep. We used to go camping on Gower, my friends and I, and later on I used the area in several of my stories, Rhosili and Worm's Head in particular.

My mother's sister, Aunt Annie, and her husband Jim farmed in Carmarthenshire, a small, run-down place known as Fern Hill. Annie and Jim weren't much good as farmers and he drank a bit, so they said.

Run-down it may have been but it was still a magical place to visit, to spend the summers, and I wrote about the place in several of my short stories. I loved the fields and the old hay barns. And the house itself – said to be where the Carmarthen hangman once lived – was spooky enough to interest any young child. The farm of Fern Hill is the subject of what many people still call my finest poem.

I have always liked writing about my childhood. The memories are always there, driving the words. So Cwmdonkin Park, my friends and family, the things I did – or imagined I did – have always inspired me. As long as I can take centre stage. I suppose I only have one subject, one topic – me. Nothing and nobody else really interests me.

Even when my father was found to have cancer of the mouth, it was the fact of his illness and possible death – in the event, he didn't die – that was most interesting to me. I was, what, eighteen years old and I was able to wallow in self-pity for weeks on end.

It was great material to write about. Because,

you see, I always knew what I wanted to be when I grew up. I wanted to be a writer.

I've always loved words. Perhaps not the meaning of them, more the sound. I suppose that came from the days before I could speak or even understand. When I was a baby, Dad used to sit by my cot and read to me – Shakespeare, Chaucer or the Bible – so the sound of those sentences filled my head long before I knew what they meant.

My father was a man of regrets. He wanted to be a poet, he wanted to be a university lecturer, he wanted to be almost anything except what he eventually became, a schoolteacher of English in a Welsh seaside town. He had a hard, bitter tongue, so his pupils respected him but were also afraid of him. So were the other teachers.

Once when I was mitching off lessons, the headmaster found me hiding in some bushes on the edge of the playground.

"What are you doing, boy?" he demanded.

"Mitching, sir," I replied.

He stared at me for a moment, wondering how to deal with such honesty.

"Well, don't let your father catch you," he said and strolled back to his office.

If even the headmaster was afraid of him, what chance did the rest of us have? Mind you, I always hated school. The early days at Mrs Hole's Dame School in Mirador Crescent, they were all right. I was the teacher's pet and I could do whatever I wanted. Like pouring water into the girls' wellington boots or peeing 'God Save the King' along the wall of the back lane. But grammar school, when I went there in 1925, that was something different.

The only thing I was any good at was English. I suppose you might expect that, with Dad being an English teacher. He was always giving me books to read and he used to mark my poems, right from the start, tell me what was good, what was poor. He didn't hold back and I soon learned to be a good judge of my own work. So English, yes. But maths and all the rest, no thank you.

Oh, there was one other thing I enjoyed. Running. I won the school mile race for the Under 15s one year. The local press made a big thing of it, even printing a photograph of me crossing the finishing line. I've got it still, over there in my wallet, in the locker where they put my things.

Proud of that win, I was. Mind you, because

I was so small and thin – you'd never believe it to look at me now – they did give me a hundred yards' head start over the rest of the field. I don't usually mention that when I tell people about my victory. See, lying again! I just can't help myself.

After that first win I took part in lots of races. And you know that story of mine, 'Extraordinary Little Cough', where a boy runs the length of Rhosili Sands? Well, I did that, several times. Running till my breath seemed to come out like steam and my chest felt like it was about to explode. But I did it, I did it. I was, I suppose, running away from everyone and everything. You could say I've been running ever since.

The room begins to fill up with people. John Berryman is there again and a tall blond man, his hair already starting to thin – John Malcolm Brinnin, the man who has organised Dylan Thomas's visits and readings in America. There are others, some of them friends, some just hangers-on, wanting to be there at the end. To be able to say 'I was there when Dylan Thomas died'.

"You'll have to be quiet," the nurse says. "If any of the doctors came in there'd be hell to pay. If you can't be quiet I'll have to ask you all to leave."

The low drum of conversation dies away and everyone stares at the man in the bed. He takes no notice of them but lies silently in his coma.

"Has anyone told his wife?" asks Berryman at last.

Brinnin nods. "Yes. I rang his London agent and told him. He's let her know what's happened. She's on her way – although God knows what she'll do when she gets here. Caitlin is, shall we say, unpredictable."

He glances across at the snub-nosed, dark-haired woman who stands alongside the poet's motionless body. She glances up at Brinnin and smiles, sadly.

"I'll be gone when she gets here," Liz Reitell whispers. "It doesn't mean I love him any less, John. If anything I love him more but nobody needs a scene, not at the moment."

"It's probably best. Caitlin is going to be hard to control – we don't need her coming face to face with his mistress."

Liz Reitell frowns, opens her mouth to speak but thinks better of it and turns back to stare at the man in the bed. She places her hand on the oxygen tent, holding it there as if the warmth from her palm can somehow get through the material and into the body of the waiting poet. "I picked a great time to fall in love," she murmurs to herself.

The door to the hospital room suddenly swings open and a black-suited man strides in. He carries a stethoscope and a brown paper file. Clearly he is a consultant and, equally clearly, he knows how to use his authority.

"What the hell is going on here? This isn't a writers' coffee morning. Don't you people realise this man is dying? Get out, now. Everyone. Get out!"

Sheepishly, knowing the doctor is right, everyone files out, leaving just him and the nurse behind. And, of course, the man in the bed.

Dying? I suppose I am. But then, I have been for years. At least that's what I always told people. A weak chest, cancer, asthma, TB, I've had them all. Lies again but, then, aren't poets always supposed to die young?

Poor Liz. Like she said, she picked a fine time to fall in love. And a fine person to do it with. I don't know if I love her in return. I think I do but I'm not sure. She was here, in New York, and I was lonely and afraid. She seemed willing to care for me and I was happy to let her do it. Love? I don't know anything much about that. Apart from Cat, you could say the only person I have ever really loved is me.

I don't suppose I've known an awful lot in my life but I did know, from an early age, that further education, university and all that, wasn't for me. Why would I want to listen to other people ranting on when I could do enough of that for myself? So, as soon as I could, I left school.

"Waste!" my father screamed when we discussed it – although discussion is hardly the word to describe the conversation. "What a waste!"

He was so angry he seemed to be jumping up and down. Mam put her hand on his arm, trying to calm him, but he just shrugged her away. He pointed at me, dangerously.

"There's thousands out there who would die for the chances you've had!"

" 'If they would rather die'," I quoted with a shrug, " 'they had better do it and decrease the surplus population'."

For a moment I thought he would explode. Then I saw the bright flame of a twinkle in his eye. Quoting Charles Dickens at him had been risky but this time, at least, it seemed to have been successful. Mam saw the change in him too.

"There now, dear," she said. "That's right. You know there's no point shouting. The boy will leave school and go to the *Post* and everything will be all right."

I sat up at that. The *Post*? Did she mean the *South Wales Evening Post*, the local paper? Dad nodded, grinning now.

"Oh yes, young man. As you know, the editor Mr Williams and I are friends. We had a little talk last night when I met him in the Uplands Hotel. Next Monday you will start in the readers' room of the paper and, with luck, you will move on to being a reporter, a journalist. You want to be a writer? Well this, young Dylan, is your chance."

I was horrified. Of course I wanted to be a writer but a proper writer, a poet or a novelist. Not some two-bit reporter on a second-rate local paper. It was no use. Argue as I might, my fate was determined and so I became a journalist.

It was boring, soul-destroying, doing the rounds of church bazaars and coffee mornings, making endless lists of all those who'd sent flowers at funerals. And as for my fellow reporters, they were a hopeless lot. I was the only one who even knew the rules of English grammar.

Mind you, I did enjoy strutting around the town, hat pulled down low across my eyes and coat collar turned up. In an old cricket shirt, dyed dark green, and with Nancy's scarf as a tie, I gave a pretty good impression of the hard-bitten reporter or news hound. Except there were no murders to write about, just local cricket matches and amateur dramatic shows.

Looking back, I can't say I learned much from my time on the paper. Perhaps the only thing of lasting importance was how to put a Woodbine in my mouth and smoke it without ever taking it out and without choking myself. It's a habit I've kept up ever since.

The job didn't last long, twelve months or

maybe a year and a half. And at the end of that we agreed to part company. I still remember my final interview with J.D. Williams, the editor, Dad's old drinking buddy. I had been to the hospital to find out who had been admitted, who had died, and totally forgot to mention the death of the hospital's popular, long-serving matron.

"It's not good enough, Mr Thomas," old JD had said. "You don't take things seriously."

I yawned and shook my head at him. "How can I take the death of one old biddy – who should have died twenty years ago – seriously? It's boring."

"I think," he said, "things have gone far enough. You're obviously not cut out for journalism and therefore I have to let –"

"I resign," I said.

"You can't. I'm about to sack you."

"Not possible," I said. "I just resigned."

"No fear, you've been sacked."

"No I haven't. I quit first."

Like I said, we agreed to go our separate ways. Mam and Dad weren't happy but for me it meant freedom. Now I could sit in my bedroom and write what I always wanted to write – poetry. Somebody once said that I wrote almost half of my *Collected Poems* in the next few years, sitting in that tiny bedroom with the boiler grumbling away inside the cupboard and the children calling from the park outside.

They were probably right. It was a very creative time, writing in my room or gossiping in the Kardomah Cafe with friends like Dan Jones, Mervyn Levy and Fred Janes. Of course, I changed or revised (that's what poets call it when you alter a poem) most of those early verses later on but they were the start of so much of my future work. Poems came easily back then, two or three a week. Now I'm lucky if I can get two lines in a month.

It wasn't just writing them, either. After a while, I started to have poems accepted by London magazines. They didn't pay much – if anything – but at least I was appearing in print.

I won a competition run by a newspaper, the *Sunday Referee*, to have my first book published. It was called simply *Eighteen Poems* and, by the standards of poetry book sales back in the 1930s, it was a success. What I mean is it sold quite well. More importantly for me, the reviews were good, people saying that I was a new name to look out for on the literary scene. All good stuff, even if I didn't believe a word of it.

In the 1930s the only place for a budding writer was London. So that was where I went. Not full time, of course, I could never have afforded that. And Swansea seemed to have a hold on me – as if I needed the place in order to write my best work. So I was always hopping back and forth between the great city and Swansea.

In London I usually stayed with my painter friends Fred Janes and Mervyn Levy in the Earls Court part of town. They were nice clean Swansea boys, Mam thought, who'd keep me on the straight and narrow. She'd have had kittens if she'd known what we got up to. I slept on a mattress or sometimes a camp bed, covered in overcoats when it got cold. And, of course, I spent most of the day in the city pubs.

There's nothing quite like the feeling of coming home after a day's drinking with friends. Even now I get a warm glow when I think of it. Up the stairs, put a match to the gas and stare out of the window at the glowing lights of London. I climb into bed, cover myself with my coats and turn to face Mervyn.

"Sing me to sleep, Merv," I say.

He has a nice voice, has Mervyn, much better than Fred or me.

"What do you want me to sing?" he asks.

"What do you think?" shouts Fred from the kitchen where he's making coffee and putting together a plate of jam sandwiches – it's what we live on. "He wants 'Bandolero'."

It is my favourite song, 'I am the Bandolero'. And whenever Mervyn gets to the line I like best – 'I am waiting and watching, an outlaw defiant' – I make him stop and repeat it three or four times.

"Don't you ever get tired of hearing that song?" asks Mervyn. "I could sing you something else, if you like."

I shake my head.

"No. I want 'Bandolero'. I can't go to sleep unless I hear it."

"He'll never tire of the damned thing," says Fred. "He thinks he's a flaming outlaw."

London, its streets paved with poems – I think that's a line from one of my stories – was a wonderful place for any young man. I can't say I wrote much when I was there but I did drink a lot. No, hang on, that's not really true. I said I was going to be honest, so let me try.

Despite what people believe, I was never a great drinker in those early days. A pint or two and that was enough for me. I could make a bottle of Bass last all evening. Other people got drunk but I just played the part. Let's say that I was always a great actor, so most people never knew. The drunker they became, the wilder and more way-out my behaviour got. We used to play a game. No – I'll tell the truth, like I said I would. *I* used to play a game.

"Little dogs, Dylan," somebody would say.

I didn't need asking again. Down on all fours I would go and spend the next half hour biting people's ankles and pretending to pee against their legs. Everyone thought it very funny but it was dangerous sometimes. Once I bit a metal lamp post and chipped my front tooth. The chip's still there, if you want to look.

Playing the part of the drunken poet wasn't easy. You could never switch off in case someone caught you out – I think that's one of the reasons why I used to run back to Swansea so often. It was all a terrible strain. I remember once walking down the street with some friends. I was going on and on about something or other, I really can't remember what. And then, for no clear reason, I just stopped. "Somebody's boring me," I said. "I think it's me."

After that I shut up and didn't speak for an

hour. My friends said it was like the calm after a storm. It didn't last, of course.

The important thing was to be the centre of attention. It's still the same. I can't help it, it just comes naturally. I've always been like that, wanting everything to circle around me. Comes of being spoiled by my Mam when I was young, I suppose. As a teenager and then as a poet in London and elsewhere, things weren't any different. Me, me, me, always me.

It was all part of the image, the wild and woolly poet. I suppose as I got older I did drink more, especially over here in America where the whiskey is cheap and the bars are open all day long. But in London, when I first went there, I didn't drink half as much as everyone thought. So there you are, one truthful story, at least.

From outside the hospital bedroom comes the sound of shouting and screaming. To begin with it's a long way away but the sounds get closer by the second. The crash of breaking glass echoes down the corridor, then the high screech of a woman's voice.

"Isn't that bloody man dead yet?"

The door smashes back against the wall and a flame-haired woman, angry, frightened and fuelled by alcohol, storms into the room. Brinnin and the others follow in her wake.

"He's very ill, Caitlin," Brinnin says. "We shouldn't disturb him."

"Disturb him?" Caitlin shouts. "I'll bloody disturb him."

She storms to the bed, tearing at the side of the oxygen tent in her fury while everyone falls back and watches her perform.

"Get up, you lazy bugger!" she shouts. "Get up! I know your tricks, always after attention, wanting to be mothered. Get up, you gutless creature."

She spins around and screams at Brinnin and all the other people in the room.

"It's all your fault! You brought him here, promised him money and fame. Didn't you know? They're the worst things you could have

23

given him. He can't cope with either of them. You've killed him as surely as if you put a gun to his head and shot him."

She sobs, wiping her arm across her eyes and leaving black marks of mascara on her cheek. Her voice is suddenly soft and low.

"Oh, John, why did you do this to him? Why couldn't you have just left him at home with his poems?"

John Brinnin moves forward, takes her arm and tries to move her away. Caitlin will have none of it. Her fist lashes out and Brinnin falls back, clutching his face. Another woman, clearly Caitlin's friend and partner in drink, raises her hands in triumph.

"Go for the jugular, baby!" she shouts.

Suddenly chaos fills the room. Caitlin is screaming, people are shouting and pushing at each other in a wave of panic. Bottles and tables are overturned and from far away comes the sound of an alarm buzzer. Security guards storm into the room, one of them holding a strait jacket, and Caitlin and her friend are led away. Only the figure in the bed lies silent and still, unmoved by what has just gone on.

"Dylan!" Caitlin shouts from the corridor outside. "Wake up, Dylan. I know what you're after. It won't work, Dylan, not this time. Wake up, you bastard!"

Her voice grows fainter and fainter. The room clears. John Brinnin holds a handkerchief to his bleeding face and follows everyone to the door. He pauses, looks back at Dylan in his bed and then goes out. The silence is like a glove.

That's my Cat. What a great line – "Isn't that bloody man dead yet?" I don't know if she was trying to shock me into waking up or if she really has had enough. I got a letter from her just a week ago, saying it was all over, that she couldn't go on. She couldn't cope with the lack of money, she said, all the drinking and the other women. She's told me that before, many times, but for some reason this time seemed different. This time it seemed final.

I have to admit, there have been other women, particularly over here in America, but then she's not exactly been innocent herself on that score. Me? I just can't seem to help myself. I get lonely and then I need comfort. That's where people like Liz come in. But I need Caitlin too. She's been a big part of my life and if she leaves me, if she walks away, there doesn't seem much point in carrying on.

I can still remember the day I first met her. It was early in 1936, in the Wheatsheaf, an old-fashioned pub just north of Oxford Street. It was a drinking hole I often used, me and lots of other writers, painters and so on. What was the name they gave the area? Oh yes, Bloomsbury, a romantic name for a pretty seedy area.

I walked into the bar that spring morning

and there was Augustus John, the painter. He was a famous face in those days, the greatest painter of the age. And, of course, he was Welsh, so we had something in common.

"Dylan," he called, "come over here. There's someone I want you to meet."

The one thing I liked about old Augustus was his sense of fun. So I thought, well, if he's got someone or something to show me I'll take a look.

"This," he said, "is Caitlin Macnamara."

He stood to one side and there, leaning against the bar, was this beautiful, golden-haired creature. She was stunning, built like a classical Greek statue. I think I fell in love that instant. I could hardly speak – unusual for me – so we stood there and drank. Well, she drank, I just stared. Until at last Augustus decided he'd had enough; it was time to go.

"We'll meet again, Dylan," Caitlin whispered, her voice low and inviting with just the faintest hint of an Irish accent. "Soon, I hope."

"Not for a while," said Augustus, his eyes glaring at me. He had already noticed her interest – and mine. "We're off to west Wales for a few weeks. Perhaps when we get back."

"Whereabouts?" I asked. "Which part of Wales?"

Augustus took Caitlin's arm and guided her towards the door. She laughed, a loud ringing tone like a cathedral bell.

"Laugharne," she called as Augustus hurried her through the doorway. "You know it?"

Then they were gone. Laugharne? Oh, I knew it well. Lots of my relatives came from down that way, Mam's family in the main. All a bit mad, there being so much in-breeding in those far-away country places. Laugharne? Well, I decided then and there, if that's where Augustus and Caitlin were going, then that's where I'd go, too.

And so I followed them. They were stopping at Laugharne Castle, where the writer Richard Hughes had a house. I got my painter friend Fred Janes to drive me and you should have seen old Augustus's face when we arrived. Furious? Not the word for it. But things seemed to settle down and after a while we all went out for a tour around the area in a great long convoy of cars – and then Fred's car broke down.

"You can come in with us, Dylan," Caitlin purred.

We left poor old Fred with his conked-out

car and I climbed into the back of Augustus's expensive motor. We spent the trip, Cat and me, cuddling there on the back seat, covered in travelling rugs, while Augustus glared at us in the rear view mirror. Thank goodness the rugs were covering us, I always said, otherwise he'd have had a heart attack.

He did have something of a turn, mind you, when we stopped for a drink at a pub outside Carmarthen. We'd had a few beers and were on our way back out of the pub when he suddenly whirled around to face me.

"Right, Thomas," he roared. "It's gone far enough, you little shit! Put your fists up."

I started to laugh but he was serious. So I did my best boxing pose, just like Jimmy Wilde or Jack Petersen. And then he hit me. Next thing I know I'm lying in the dusty car park and Augustus is driving off in a cloud of smoke and glory. According to some of my friends who saw them drive away, Caitlin was grinning like the cat that got the cream. Having men fight over her always made her smirk like that.

Getting thumped by Augustus John didn't put me off. If anything, it made me more determined to make her a part of my life. So I just kept chasing her. Wherever Caitlin was you could be sure that, within a day or so, I'd be there. She seemed to like being chased – at least she didn't complain – and a year later we were married. In Cornwall, of all places. And Augustus gave us his blessing.

Mam and Dad knew nothing about it, not till it was too late. Dad was so angry – foolish young people, he called us – but he still sent me five pounds when he heard the news. It was money he couldn't really afford but I took it. Anything to keep poverty from the door. After a while Caitlin and I went to Swansea to stay with Mam and Dad, then to her parents in Hampshire.

How can I describe our marriage? Stormy. That's a good-enough description. We fought and, I can tell you, Caitlin was a good fighter, as good as Augustus John, I reckon. A hell of a lot better than me. It didn't stop me trying, though I was always better with words than my fists. She could pick me up and tuck me under her arm in those days. I'd like to see her do it now that I've put on so much weight – filled out, as we say in Wales.

It didn't take much to start an argument. A bit of stupidity from one or other of us and we'd be off, ready to kill each other. I know, a lot of the time, it was my fault. Cat made the mistake of telling me, once, that her father had said women were a blank sheet of paper for men to write on. I used to throw that one at her all the time. Oh boy, would she get angry.

There were so many other reasons to fight. Not that we needed reasons. We'd fight over nothing, at the drop of a hat, as my mother used to say.

Imagine the scene. It's a Saturday night and my friend the poet Vernon Watkins has come to visit. We've only got one bed so he'll have to share with Cat and me – but we won't tell him till later. A bit straight is Vernon, had a nervous breakdown a few years ago. It doesn't take much to push him over the edge. Anyway, he's come to see us.

"Brought you some plums," says Vernon, offering Caitlin a brown paper bag.

I'm lying on the bed – like I say, the only bed we've got.

"Give me a plum, Cat," I say, holding out my hand.

She ignores me. And so I start to whine at her.

"Cat, Cat, please, give me a plum."

She shakes her head and turns her back on

31

me, but I really do want a plum so I keep on. And on, and on. Once I've started I just can't seem to stop.

"Cat, darling, lovely Cat, give Dylan a plum."

At last she whirls round and responds.

"You want a plum, Dylan, come and get one."

It's like a red rag to a bull. There is no way I'm going to get up off the bed and go to her, that would mean she'd won. And so I keep on, whining and asking her to pass me a plum. And eventually she cracks.

"You want a plum? Here."

And she throws one at me, hits me smack on the forehead. Caitlin likes that, thinks it's funny, so she throws another. And another. Soon the whole bag is flying towards me and I'm covered in sticky plum juice. Then she storms out into the garden. I manage to find a whole plum, a more or less whole plum, and start to eat it. I know there'll be hell to pay later but for the moment it's over.

"That's sorted that out," I tell Vernon. "Now let's talk poetry."

I think it was the spring of 1938 that we first moved to Laugharne to live, in a little cottage called Eros on the road out of town to the south. Laugharne was – still is – a strange place, full of half-mad, half-witted fighters and brawlers. Saturday night in the main street, after the pubs closed, was like the Wild West – Wyatt Earp would have felt at home there.

I've heard what they say, that Laugharne was the model for Llareggub, the town in my play *Under Milk Wood*. I wouldn't agree with that but it did play a part. So did New Quay. Ask any writer and he'll tell you his places and his people are made up from several different sources. So it was with Llareggub. You've picked up the joke with that name, haven't you? If not, try spelling it backwards, see what you get.

After a few months in Eros, Cat and I moved to Sea View, a much bigger, grander house, closer to the centre of the village. We had no money and lived mainly on cockle stew – cockles that Cat gathered from the seashore – and on bottles of stout from Brown's Hotel just down the road. We used tea chests as tables and as there was no electricity we had candles stuck onto saucers or in empty beer bottles to give light. It was all pretty basic and we loved it.

I suppose we should have been quite well off. My second book, *Twenty Five Poems*, had come out. But it didn't sell as well as my first one – people complained that it was full of complex poems that nobody could understand. I couldn't blame them, I didn't understand half of them myself.

"Why don't you write something that's easy to read, something where the meaning is clear," said Caitlin. She was sitting in front of our tea-chest dining table, counting out the few pennies and sixpences we had left that week – it didn't take her long.

"Keep it simple and maybe people will buy it. We need money, Dylan."

"These stories I'm writing now," I replied, "they're pretty simple. You'd have to be an idiot not to understand them."

"So get them into a book," Cat said. "For God's sake earn us some money."

Those stories were about my childhood and they later became *Portrait of the Artist as a Young Dog*. My work was also beginning to get published in America and I was starting to write broadcasts for the BBC. That brought in a few pounds.

Even then there were a few problems with the BBC. I was never much good at hitting deadlines and several times I missed a recording.

It made them cagey about booking me or, rather, paying in advance, but they liked the sound of my voice and they kept on using me. So we should have been all right.

But we weren't. Money came in and we spent it. Sometimes we spent it before it even came in. Anyway, debts were mounting – we must have owed money to every tradesman in the village. The one thing you can't do in a small place like Laugharne is not pay your debts. It's OK to have them but you must pay up when the time comes. Except, of course, that was something we couldn't do.

And then the war came. With Hitler in charge in Germany, everyone had been expecting war for years but when it was finally declared in September 1939 it seemed to take the whole world by surprise. It was the perfect time to do a bunk.

The hospital room is as silent as the tomb. In the bed Dylan is lying quietly. His breathing is shallow, almost non-existent, breaths that hardly lift or flutter his chest. His face is chalky white and shines like a clean bed-sheet in the gloom of the hospital room. His eyes are open but do not seem able to focus on anything.

Liz Reitell ghosts in through the doorway, carefully shutting the door behind her. She drops into a chair alongside the bed, her head buried in her hands.

"Are you going to sit with him for a while?" asks the nurse. "I need to make a phone call. I'll only be gone a few minutes."

Liz nods her head. "I'm not going anywhere," she says. She stares at the figure in the bed, an unbroken glare, as if she is willing him to wake up and speak. She knows it will not happen but it does not stop her trying.

John Malcolm Brinnin enters the room and walks to her side.

"No change?" he asks.

There is no need for an answer. Brinnin puts his hand on her shoulder.

"Caitlin saw you," he says, "just before they took her away."

"Really?"

"She swore and screamed, no more than you'd expect. They've taken her to Rivercrest, a private hospital across the river. It was either that or get her committed to Bellevue, the city mental hospital. It's probably for the best – she tried to throw herself out of a window just now."

"Poor woman," says Liz. She points at the silent figure on the bed. "He seems to have a habit of hurting people, even when he's not trying."

Brinnin says nothing. He knows she is right. He knows that Caitlin, like Liz and so many others – like himself and John Berryman, come to that – has been under Dylan's spell for a long time now. It's a spell that even death will not change.

They fall into silence as the long shadows of evening begin to stretch like ghostly fingers across the floor. Liz Reitell cries quietly to herself and Brinnin watches.

Don't cry, Liz. You couldn't have done anything to help me, to save me, I should say. Once the past started to die on me, I had nothing left to write about. And after that I was always heading only one way – to the grave.

The past, my past, really started to go when the Germans bombed Swansea in February 1941. I remember standing on the corner of High Street where Ben Evans Department Store used to be, on the morning after the last raid. All I could see were burnt-out buildings and the firemen's hoses that ran like giant snakes amongst the rubble. Caitlin and my old friend Bert Trick were with me.

Bert was an old-fashioned socialist who was also a bit of a poet. He had tried hard to teach me about politics but it was no use, I wasn't really interested. So he gave up and we just used to talk about poetry instead.

Come to think of it, that morning after the raid in Swansea was the last time I ever saw Bert. We used to be so close in the years just after I left school, but time and events pushed us apart. And like I say, I haven't seen him since that morning.

"This is what war does, young Thomas," he called when he first saw me picking my way down the rubble-strewn roadway. "Destroys everything."

He caught my arm and dragged me towards the remains of Evans's Department Store.

"Man's inhumanity to man," he said.

It was hardly original, a bit like Bert's poetry, I suppose. But then, I wasn't friendly with him because I liked his work. It was the man I admired.

"Terrible," he kept saying. "Terrible, terrible."

"Our Swansea is dead, Bert," I said.

He thought I was just being my normal poetic self – whatever that might be – but I meant it. The Swansea we had known was gone, smashed away in those terrible three nights of bombing. All the shops and stores, the grammar school, even the Kardomah Cafe, all gone. And from that point on everything began to unravel. Me and Cat, arguments that suddenly weren't fun any more, her affairs – and mine.

And it all came to an end, a climax you could say, when Dad died. He'd been such a constant figure in my life, my past, and now that past was well and truly over.

But I'm getting ahead of myself. Typical Welsh, gabbling on at full speed. Slow down, there's more to be told, a lot more. And there's still time yet.

Cat always said that the best thing to come out of our relationship was the kids – Llewelyn, Aeronwy and Colm. She was probably right but that didn't stop her resenting them. They tied her down, kept her at home being a mother, while I was gallivanting around the country doing – well, doing what wild Welsh poets should do. She was always wilder and more fun-loving than me. And she wanted a piece of it all – except that she couldn't get it because of the children.

The war years were the worst for her. They turned me down for the army, thank God, said I wasn't fit enough to become a soldier. It was a load off my mind, I can tell you. I didn't fancy trotting about with a gun and getting shot at for my pains.

I was thinking of declaring myself a conscientious objector but then I had this medical and the ruling about my fitness and health saved me the problem. I didn't know how we were going to live because the war had cut me off from lots of people and places that used to give me money. It was a worrying time for a while.

I didn't know it then, but the answer to all our problems was just around the corner. My life was about to change. In 1942 I got a job writing scripts for a company called Strand Films.

"They want my company to produce films for the Ministry of Information," Donald Taylor, the owner of Strand Films, told me when we first met – in a pub in London, of course. "Nothing too grand, just short things, ten or fifteen minutes long, for showing before the main features and after the Pathe News."

"I love the cinema," I said, "but I've never written a film script in my life. I wouldn't know where to start."

Taylor shrugged. "You'll learn. All you need are lots of nice images – anti-aircraft guns, balloon sites, bomb damage, that type of thing – and some of your rolling Welsh descriptions. They want to get the message across – Britain can take it."

He grinned at me, nudged me in the ribs. "Who knows what it might lead on to? I want to make feature films, for the cinema. Got this idea for a film about Burke and Hare, the body snatchers. You could do a great script for that. And who knows, maybe we'll turn one of your stories into a film. All after the war, of course. For now, it's just information films for the government."

I wasn't sure and told him so. But then came the clincher.

"We'll pay you ten pounds a week."

After that it was a done deal. I accepted and was put on the payroll. I must have worked on a dozen films during the war, writing the scripts, doing voice-overs, even directing. It meant I had to be in London quite often while Caitlin stayed at home with the children.

Home? It was a lot of different places in those early war years after we'd left Laugharne. Sometimes with her mother in Hampshire, sometimes in Swansea or with friends in Gloucester. And, towards the end of the war, in a bungalow in New Quay on the Cardiganshire coast. I joined her when I could, usually when I was tired or when the money ran out.

I enjoyed film work. I must admit, to begin with I didn't think I would, but once I learned what I had to do it was fun. Not too taxing on the brain, just using my ability with words. And it was, strangely, good to feel part of the war effort. We were helping to keep up morale in the public, in its way as important as throwing a hand grenade or firing an ack-ack gun. Caitlin, of course, hated it.

"You're wasting your talent!" she screamed. "You should be writing poems, not stupid lines for a film that nobody will ever watch or listen to."

"I enjoy it," I countered.

She got really angry at that. "Enjoy it? You enjoy being idle. You know you can churn that stuff out in your sleep. You're betraying your talent, your skill. You've sold out, Dylan."

Truth be known, it was something of a relief, not having to write poems or stories every week. The pressure was off. I couldn't say that to Caitlin, so I tried to tell her that it was a job, the first full-time and regular job I'd had since I left the *South Wales Evening Post*. And it was bringing in money, a good wage.

"A good wage?" she hollered. "With me stuck out in the country and you in London, most of it's spent long before it gets to me."

She had a point. Mind you, I'm sure that's what her argument was really all about, the fact that we were often living in two different places. It wasn't about me wasting my talent, far from it. She was stuck with the kids – only two of them at that stage but Colm, the youngest, would arrive soon – while I was doing the rounds of the pubs in London.

"I'll try to spend less," I said. "And get down to see you more often."

She glared at me, as if I didn't understand. "Never mind you coming to see me, what about me coming up to London a bit more often."

And so we got a studio apartment in Chelsea. Llewelyn stayed with Cat's mother in Hampshire but the baby had to come with us. The apartment was dirty and the roof leaked – we had to put an umbrella over Aeronwy's cot to keep the water off her face. But with my books and a gramophone we made the place feel like home. I can still smell the warm rich aroma of the stews Caitlin made in that tiny place. Wonderful what she could do with a few potatoes and a little bit of meat – the Irish in her, I suppose.

Cat loved it, of course, not just the studio but the whole atmosphere of war-time London. All the uniforms and the café life, the pubs full to bursting and dozens of men and women enjoying the experience while there was still time.

It was too good to last. When the flying bombs started landing on London in 1943 or

1944 we left the city again. But Cat had had her moment in the sun. I don't say she was happy to go but she accepted that it wasn't safe in London any more.

Night has come and darkness fills the hospital room. The visitors and watchers – Liz Reitell, John Brinnin, John Berryman and the rest – have left. Some have gone back to their homes or hotels to sleep or rest, to prepare for more waiting and watching tomorrow. Some, like Brinnin and Reitell, doze in the hospital waiting room, not wanting to be too far away, in case they are suddenly called or needed during the night.

Now, tonight, it is the silence that dominates the room. It fills every corner, lying like an invisible mist over the equipment, chairs and tables. Outside the window, even the normal hum of New York city has died away – no sirens or car horns wailing, no traffic roaring past, no calls and cries from the alleyways. And for those not used to it the effect is sudden and startling.

Tonight, only the ever-present nurses remain alert and awake. Like sentries on guard they enter and leave the room in a routine, eternal patrol. They come and go in regular shifts, check sheets and forms, make comments or marks on charts. When they meet, at the doorway or at the foot of the bed, they exchange low comments in whispers.

The man in the bed, the poet, is speechless, as he has been since he was admitted. His eyes flicker open, then close. Whatever happens in the room makes no difference to him. He is beyond it all. He is waiting to die.

Of course I'm not waiting to die. I know it will happen, probably sooner rather than later, but don't ever say that I'm lying here, just waiting for the end. No, there's so much to think through.

I'm not looking forward to it, death. What did someone once say? That I loved graveyards but feared death? That's pretty accurate. So, although I know there's no point in going on, and although I know I've reached the end – my end, anyway – I can't say I'm looking forward to what's out there, in the great beyond, as romantic novelists would say.

We had a good run, Caitlin and me, but I think the war years finally put the nail in our coffin – God, I am full of clichés tonight. It doesn't matter. For the first time in my life the meaning of the words is more important than their sound. There's still so much I want to say.

I can't remember exactly when we moved to Majoda, a small bungalow on the cliffs outside New Quay in Cardiganshire. It was the winter of 1944, I think, and the bungalow was built of wood and bits of tin. So it was damned cold in there. No heating apart from a paraffin stove, and water had to be collected from a tap on the main road. We rented it for a pound a week.

Donald Taylor had called it a day with Strand Films but he wasn't finished with cinema. He formed another company, Gryphon Films, and had plans to make proper films, proper feature-length films for general release. As far as I was concerned it meant that, as well as poems and other things, I was also working on some film scripts while we were living at Majoda. Which didn't please Caitlin at all. In her eyes Taylor was a crook and a con man. And it meant that I was often called back to London – leaving her stranded on the Cardiganshire cliffs.

On one of my visits I was supposed to be best man at Vernon Watkins's wedding. I didn't turn up. No excuses but, well, at least it was a new slant on the old joke about the bride not arriving at the church. Poor Vernon, he shouldn't have asked me. Caitlin knew that.

"You're making a big mistake, Vernon," she told him. "He'll probably forget to turn up."

"He'll be OK," Vernon replied. "He's my best friend. How could I get married and not have him as best man? He'll be fine on the day."

"Have you ever seen him at a proper, formal do?"

Vernon shook his head. "No, but I'm sure he'll be fine."

"Don't say you haven't been warned," Cat said. "It will be a disaster."

She was right, of course. She was very right. When I failed to show up for the wedding, Vernon threatened never to forgive me but he did, in the end. I really don't know why I missed the ceremony. I just think it was all beyond me, all that formality, the speeches and the like.

Back in Majoda life went on. By March 1945 an old friend of ours, Vera Killick – I had known her in school in Swansea, Vera Phillips as she was then – was living in another bungalow just along the cliff from us with her baby. Cat and I had become quite friendly with Vera when we met again in London and we stayed friends when we moved back to Wales.

"And William," says Caitlin. "Don't forget William."

It's not really Caitlin, of course, more a distant voice in my ear. But whether it's Cat or just my imagination, she's right. William, Vera's husband, was a typical product of the war, an army captain, a commando, a man trained to fight and operate as a lethal killing machine.

"Dangerous man," says Cat. "A highly dangerous man."

All right, all right. I know how dangerous he

was. Earlier on in the war, we'd spent time, the four of us, in a house at Tal-sarn on the road between Aberaeron and Lampeter. It was soon after they got married. Then William was sent away.

"To war," says Cat. "He went to war."

See the criticism? Happens all the time. William went to war, I didn't. She had never wanted me to go off to fight but she still can't help putting the knife in.

The problems started when Captain William Killick, commando and soldier of the King, came back from the fighting. He'd spent nearly two years behind enemy lines in Greece. God knows what he'd seen and done. And when he came back he was in a pretty bad way.

"So would you be," Cat hisses. "You and your chicken bones, breaking every time you fall out of bed!"

"I'm not talking about physical damage, Cat. I mean his mental state."

Cat snorts. "Hah. Don't talk to me about mental states. At least he had a real reason to be disturbed – not like some people I could mention."

William was very shaken up after his Greek experience. We'd always got on quite well – I remember our time at Tal-sarn with real affection. We used to wheel Aeronwy's pram back from the pub, full to the brim with bottles of beer, and then sit and drink them together. Mind you, even then he used to get very aggressive when he'd had a drink. Me, I just went stupid.

"Good word, stupid," says Cat. "For you, anyway. Get on with the story."

After he came back things were strained between us. He was short-tempered and seemed to take a dislike to me. He was always picking faults.

"Can you blame him?" sneers Cat. "Him out there facing all sorts of dangers. The worst thing you had to face was a broken beer bottle."

"All right, Cat, I'm just painting in the background."

A few days after his return William was called in to see his bank manager. It seemed that Vera had run up a pretty big overdraft. She'd been very generous to Cat and me – yes, Cat, to both of us – always handing out loans. And, like us, she'd got used to drinking a lot. So she was happily spending William's army pay while he was out in Greece risking his life for King and country.

"Berserk," says Caitlin, "he went berserk, accused Vera of all sorts – including having an affair with you. What a joke that was. She wouldn't have looked twice at an under-sized shrimp like you."

Caitlin's right, of course she is. They had a terrible row and Vera took the baby and went off to her mother's, leaving William behind in their bungalow. He was upset, obviously, and went into New Quay and started drinking. Rum, I think he was on. By evening, when he staggered into the Commercial pub, he was well gone.

"That's when you ignored him," says Cat.

"I didn't ignore him," I protest. "I was with some film people from Gryphon Films. They'd come down from London to see me and we were talking about a script they wanted me to write. I just didn't see him."

"He soon put a stop to that, didn't he?"

Cat's right. He came over to our table and started ranting on about how we were too high and mighty to talk to him and how none of us knew what it was like "out there". He ended up slapping one of the film people, a woman called Fanya Fisher. I got in between them and we threw a few punches at each other.

"Oh yeah?" says Cat. "I'd have loved to see that. He could have picked you up in one hand and squeezed you dry like an orange."

She can say what she likes, we did fight. We were both pretty drunk, which is probably why there was no real damage to either of us but, when we were separated, William was thrown out of the pub. I had a few more drinks and then I went back to Majoda. There seemed to be lots of people in the house that night, visitors and locals alike. And there were also a couple of babies – Aeronwy being one of them – sleeping in one of the bedrooms.

I don't know what was going through his mind but William, over in his bungalow, decided it was time to give us all a real taste of war. He picked up his Sten gun and walked over to Majoda. He stood outside and loosed off a couple of bursts. The place was just a shack and the shots went right through the walls.

"The bullets missed Aeronwy by inches," says Cat. "Your fault – if you hadn't ignored him he'd never have done it."

Thanks, Cat, just can't leave it, can you? Everyone dropped to the floor. Then came more firing and William burst in through the door. He was waving his gun about and threatening to kill us all. He fired another burst into the ceiling, then I took his gun off him. That makes it sound a lot more dramatic than it really was. In fact he was quite happy to hand over the Sten – all the energy seemed to have gone out of him. It didn't stop me shaking with fear, facing down a man with a loaded gun.

"I suppose I'll have to give you that," says Cat. "It was the bravest thing I ever saw you do. The only brave thing in fact."

William had a hand grenade as well. He threatened to blow us all to Hell if we didn't give him his gun back. So I gave him the gun and someone walked him home to his bungalow along the cliff. I think the police arrived later on and took him into custody.

"There was a trial," says Caitlin. "But the judge dismissed the case. He took one look at you and decided William would have been better off if he had shot you."

He was shooting at all of us, Cat, not just me. All of us. But she's right, the judge did decide that, in view of Captain Killick's war record – and my lack of one – there was no case to answer. I suppose that was a fairly accurate judgement.

It is morning at last. A grey half-light creeps through the grimy windows into the hospital room as the nurses move around switching off the electric ceiling lights, smoothing down the bed-clothes, checking the charts. From the corridor outside comes the clatter of breakfast dishes and the cheery calls of ward orderlies.

John Malcolm Brinnin and Liz Reitell come in through the door and move carefully to the bed. They are sleepy and their clothes are untidy, the result of spending the night in hospital chairs. They stare down at Dylan.

"No change," says Liz.

It is not a question, just a statement of fact. Brinnin reaches out to comfort her but she shakes her head and sits in the chair close to Dylan's face. For ten long minutes there is no sound, no movement in the room. Liz stares at her lover and Brinnin bites his thumbnail, staring at the floor.

"I'm just so glad his play went well," says Liz.

Brinnin is lost in his own thoughts and doesn't reply. Liz tries again.

"The play, *Under Milk Wood*. It went well, didn't it, John?"

Brinnin nods. "Yes, very well. People seemed

to love it. He was nervous about it, you know, didn't know if it was what he wanted to say, didn't know how the audience would react."

"He was always nervous, every time he read or spoke in public."

She stops, suddenly. "Listen to me, already talking about him in the past tense. As if he's already dead."

"I find myself doing the same thing," says John Brinnin. "I was thinking, last night when I was lying there half asleep in the waiting room, of the last thing he ever said to me. It was at the party after the first performance of *Milk Wood*. He came up behind me, put his arms around me tightly and whispered in my ear – 'You do know this is for ever, don't you, John.' It was as if he knew what was coming, knew that he wouldn't survive much longer."

Liz smiles, sadly. "I doubt if people will remember that as his last line in years to come. They're far more likely to remember that bloody silly lie he told me."

Brinnin stares at her, questioning.

"He went out, the day before he collapsed. Came back and told me, 'I've had eighteen straight whiskies. I think that's the record'. He couldn't resist exaggerating the truth."

"It's the sort of epitaph he'd want," says Brinnin. "But you know and I know that eighteen whiskies would have killed him."

"It probably has," says Liz.

"Probably has what?"

"Killed him."

They stare at each other, suddenly conscious of what Liz has said. She sobs loudly. It is as if a dam has been broken. She throws herself into Brinnin's arms and they hold each other, long and hard. The figure on the bed does not move.

OK, guys, if we're talking about *Under Milk Wood* there's a few things that need to be made clear. One, it's a piece of hack work, pulp fiction, not in the same league as my poems – even though it's what most people will remember me for. And two, it began life long before those performances in America in 1953.

You know what *Milk Wood* is about, don't you? Twenty-four hours, night and day, in the life of a town that is barking mad. All the people – policemen, retired sea captains, butchers, bakers, the lot – all as mad as hatters. It was an idea I had been thinking about for years.

I started writing radio scripts – monologues they'd be called now – back in the war years. One of those broadcasts was called *Quite Early One Morning* and it describes a town, an imaginary town – even though it does sound a bit like New Quay – and the goings-on of the men and women who live there. What's that if it's not the beginnings of *Milk Wood* taking shape in my head?

Then there was a documentary I made for the BBC after the war, called *The Londoner*. Nobody remembers it now but it described a day in the life of a London street, twenty-four hours of the lives of ordinary working-class people. See, *Under Milk Wood* again.

After the war Caitlin, the children and I lived a vagabond life. We were with my parents for a while. They'd sold Cwmdonkin Drive and moved to Blaen Cwm, just across the water from Laugharne. It was where so many of our ancestors came from but it was too Welsh, too tight, for me. In 1946 we moved to South Leigh in Oxfordshire.

"Bloody Margaret Taylor," says Cat in my ear, in my head.

"She was good to us," I counter. "Let us have that house in South Leigh for a pittance of a rent. I don't know how we'd have managed if she hadn't helped us out."

Cat snorts. Well, it sounds like a snort. That's the trouble lying here like this, flat on your back and not moving, you're never really sure about the noises in your head.

"Miss grand, hoity toity," says the voice of Cat. "Her and that stuffed shirt husband of hers."

Now there I do agree with Cat. I never liked A.J.P. Taylor, the historian. It was before he became a famous face on television, the country's popular historian. Then he was just a history lecturer at one of the Oxford colleges. I always felt he was looking down his nose at me. He resented Margaret supporting me, helping me out like she did. He thought I was taking advantage of her – which, of course, I was.

But I enjoyed Oxford. It was close enough for me to get into London whenever I needed, whenever the BBC wanted me to record a programme. And after the publication of my new book – *Deaths and Entrances*, a huge success, even if I do say so myself – I began to get more and more BBC work.

"Make sure you get there," Caitlin would say as she saw me off for another trip to London. "We need the cash."

The BBC had got a bit stroppy after I failed to turn up a few times, wouldn't pay until after I'd done the job. So Cat was right to remind me.

"Of course I'll get there," I would usually counter – and then add, under my breath, "It's getting back you should be worried about."

The critics said that *Deaths and Entrances* marked a new direction in my poetry. It was more easily understood now, poems like 'Fern Hill' taking centre stage. Some of my radio broadcasts from this time – and you can't get more direct than them – were later published as books. Pieces like *Return Journey*, *A Visit to Grandpa's* and *A Child's Christmas in Wales* were more successful and made more money than all my poetry put together.

"Tell them about Italy," says Cat in my head.

Well, she would want that, wouldn't she. For her, Italy was a place of pure enjoyment. As far as she was concerned, it was like walking through the gates of Paradise. Somebody once said that Italy was Caitlin's territory, not mine. A pretty accurate statement, I'd say.

In 1947 I was given a travelling scholarship from the Society of Authors – Margaret Taylor's work again – and we decided to go by train to Italy, all of us, the whole family, including Cat's sister. It was an eventful journey. I lost all our luggage at the Italian border. Well, the luggage got lost but I, of course, took the blame.

It's a long trip, Britain to northern Italy but, at last, we ended up in a villa outside Florence. The heat nearly killed me and I spent most of the next few weeks lying on my bed, curtains drawn, swigging ice cold beer straight from the bottle. I wrote almost nothing.

Cat was in her element. The sun made her skin glow and she turned the head of every man who crossed her path. You could say it was a bit of a crisis point for us. Everything changed during that Italian trip and suddenly she was the centre of attention, not me. Suddenly she was in charge.

"Too right," whispers Cat. "That was when I finally realised that I didn't need you any more. You, on the other hand, certainly did need me."

True enough. I think it was then that I first sensed she was slipping away from me. When we moved on to the island of Elba she became infatuated by an Italian café owner and fisherman. I think she actually fell in love with him.

"He was sweet," says Cat – and in my imagination I see her eyes go soft and wet. "A proper man, doing a man's job, not sweating over idiotic poems."

I was pleased when our time in Italy came to an end, even if Cat wasn't. But come to an end it did and it was back to cold, rainy Britain. Then came the problem of finding somewhere permanent to live.

I'd always had a hankering to go back to Laugharne, where Caitlin and I had lived when we were first married. I had always known that Wales was where I wrote my best work and, to be honest with you, South Leigh was a bit too close to London for comfort. Oh, it was good for the BBC but when I went up for a half-hour or twenty-minute recording, the visit always seemed to end up in a three or four day drinking session. So whatever money I made from the broadcasts soon found its way into the pockets and tills of every landlord in the city.

Laugharne had always had a real appeal for me. It was a strange little place full of strange little people – and big ones, too – who somehow managed to get into my imagination. The problem was finding a house. We had no money and if we were going to move to Laugharne it was clear that we were going to need help – patronage is a good word – from someone like Margaret Taylor.

"What I need, Margaret," I told her, "is a house with a view, close enough to town so we can walk in to buy groceries but far enough outside to keep people away."

"And what does Caitlin want?" she asked.

I shrugged. "The same as me. She knows how easily I can get distracted. She just wants a place where she can build a home for me and the children."

I don't know how Caitlin would have felt about me describing her as a home builder but Margaret Taylor seemed taken in. I laid out exactly what we wanted. It was cheeky, I know, but as I said before, let the ravens feed us. Margaret was willing to be used. I don't know why, there was never anything sexual between us – even though Cat thought there was. Perhaps she wanted to go down in history as a modern patron of the arts.

Anyway, after I'd told her what I needed to live properly and write well, Margaret Taylor agreed to go looking. And look she did.

It took time but then, in the spring or early summer of 1949, she found what she was searching for. The Boat House was not in the centre of town but it was close enough. Pinned to the cliff overlooking the river, there was also a small shed that came with the property, the ideal workplace for me. We moved there in May.

Caitlin was pregnant with our last child, Colm as we later christened him, when we moved into the Boat House. The location was wonderful and the views superb. I always said that if a man couldn't write there, he couldn't write anywhere. But the house itself was cold and damp and, to begin with, there was no mains water. And the toilet was outside!

Mam and Dad joined us in Laugharne,

moving into a terraced cottage in the main street, a place called the Pelican. I used to go there every morning to work on *The Times* crossword with Dad, then spend an hour or two across the road in Brown's Hotel. In the afternoon I'd work in the shed.

As if to celebrate my return I wrote a poem immediately we settled into the Boat House, the first poem for some time. It was called 'Over Sir John's Hill' and my good friend Vernon Watkins called it the most perfect poem I ever wrote. I think it was pretty good, too, but you don't have to look far into the thing to see that it's all about death. Perhaps, even then, I knew what was coming.

John Berryman has returned to the hospital. He doesn't know why he is so fascinated by this ending, this death. After all, he barely knows Dylan Thomas – his work, yes, the man, no. But he feels drawn to this hospital room and to the sight of the helpless poet marooned in the bed.

He stands between Liz Reitell and John Malcolm Brinnin, gazing at Thomas but feeling strangely distant. Reitell and Brinnin, he can see, are upset but he feels little more than an academic interest in the events. He wonders how much longer it can go on.

"Tell me," he says, suddenly. "All those stories about Dylan, the drinking and the womanising, the thieving and all the rest, are they true? Or just part of the Dylan-legend."

Brinnin considers carefully before replying.

"It depends. Different people see different things in him. The worst he ever did with me was steal a few of my shirts. Other people will tell you another side to the story. There's a tale about him once stealing the silver from a house where he was staying. When the owners came back they found cloths and silver polish on the sideboard. He'd cleaned the silver before he pawned it. That's the story. How true it is, I don't know. Dylan had – has – a knack of giving people what they want."

"So if you expect him to be a drunk, that's what he is. You expect him to be the perfect guest – that's how he behaves. You want a thief, he'll be a thief. Is that what you're saying?"

"Exactly. The only thing he is to everyone is the perfect poet."

Berryman nods his head and stores the information away.

"He's upset a lot of people," says Brinnin. "But I think there are people out there who encourage his bad behaviour. For some of the folk we've met in our travels it's like a badge of honour if Dylan has stolen their shirts or ties. It's like being elected to the chief club in town."

John Berryman laughs. "You two should go and have a break," he tells Liz and Brinnin. "You look exhausted, all done in. Go home and have a shower or a bath. Get a change of clothes."

Brinnin looks at Liz, eyebrows raised in question. She shakes her head.

"I'll stay, thanks. Maybe I'll go and get a coffee or some breakfast. But I'm not leaving the hospital. Not till –"

She cannot finish the sentence. Berryman shrugs his shoulders. It's up to her. He's made the offer, can't do more than that. He turns to Brinnin.

"You want to go home? Or stay here with her?"

Brinnin thinks about it. The promise of a hot shower is almost more than he can bear. But if Liz is staying, he knows it is his duty to stay with her.

"I'll keep her company," he says. "We'll get something to eat – there's a restaurant down on the next floor."

Berryman nods. "You do that. I'll come and get you if there's any change, any developments. You go and get some coffee – bring one back for me."

Brinnin smiles at him. He and Liz go out leaving Berryman and the ever-present nurse to watch over the poet in the bed. Alone in the room with the dying poet, John Berryman sits and sighs.

"So what's it all about, Dylan?" he murmurs, almost to himself. "How the hell did you end up like this? What's it all about?'

What's it all about? I'll tell you my friend, my non-friend I should say. After all, I hardly know you. And perhaps that's better for the final part of this fractured, hopeless life of mine. The final confession, I suppose.

America was always the draw. I'd thought of coming years ago, when my poetry and stories first began to sell over here. It was the land of big bucks, where the pavements – sorry, sidewalks – were lined with dollar bills. After the war I tried to get a job teaching at one of the universities but I had no luck. My reputation went before me – a drunkard, a man who can't be trusted, fat, and very, very unhealthy. At least, that's what I think was the problem.

But then, just after we'd moved into the Boat House, a letter arrived. It was always a long walk for the postman, across the cliff path and then down the steep cut back towards the house under the rocks and trees. I watched him as he picked his way along.

"American postmark, Mr Thomas," he said, offering me the flimsy piece of paper. "If you don't want it, perhaps you'd let me have the stamp? My nephew collects them."

I ripped off the corner of the envelope and passed it across. He nodded and plodded on his way. I went inside the house, to the kitchen where Cat was sitting at the table, peeling potatoes. I sat alongside her and stared at the envelope.

"Well, open it," she said, throwing another potato into the pot.

"It's from somebody called John Malcolm Brinnin," I told her, my heart already beginning to race. "He's the Director of a Poetry Centre – look how he spells it, Center – wants me to go to New York, to read poems. Do they really have Poetry Centres over there?"

Cat sneered and took the envelope from my hands. "More work for nothing? One day, Dylan, you're going to have to start earning some money."

"He's willing to pay five hundred dollars," I said before she could read Brinnin's words. "And give me the airfare."

She sat up at that but I think, even then, she was wary. She guessed it would mean her being left alone for a couple of months while I had the time of my life in the USA. She wasn't far wrong, either.

Brinnin was as good as his word. The tickets arrived and I headed off to New York knowing that he'd arranged lots of readings and talks for me in cities across the country. Each one of them meant more money. It was the gravy train.

That first trip set the tone for the three that followed. Remember, Britain was still suffering from the effects of the war. Rationing was still in place and there were bomb sites everywhere. But America? It was clean and fresh – and it was rich. Food and drink were cheap and at the White Horse Inn, down at Greenwich Village in New York, I had my first taste of Old Grand-Dad whiskey. Wow.

I suppose I went a bit wild. There were parties after every reading and drinking sessions at the White Horse and other bars. Always there were the college girls who hung on my every word, young and pretty, keen and willing – the girls, that is, not my words. I've never been able to control myself when there are goodies on offer. Cat says I've always been like a little boy in a sweet shop – I'll have one of those, one of those and so on. She's right. And that first visit to America there was so much on offer.

"I guess it's my fault," John Brinnin said to me one day.

We were in his car, sitting in a long line of traffic on the freeway. The red tail lights of the stationary cars stretched away like a trail of comets ahead of us.

"What do you mean, John?"

"The drinking and the parties, your bad behaviour. Last night in particular. All the trouble you caused."

The night before we'd been at a cocktail party and I'd been at my 'Dylan best'. I couldn't resist performing for all the academics who were there – the professors, lecturers and the like. Anything to see them shocked out of their cosy, protected lives. I drank everything and anything on offer. It finished up with me grabbing some writer woman and lifting her up so that her head hit the ceiling. There was hell to pay and we left with our tails between our legs.

"A good night," I laughed. "But I don't see how any of it was your fault."

He glanced at me before putting the car into gear and inching along a couple of feet. Then we ground to a halt again and he wrenched on the handbrake.

"Do you remember your first reading? At the Poetry Center? I introduced you, said you were a poet out of 'the druidical mists of Wales'. I reckon that gave you a licence to behave like some ancient mystical bard from foreign shores."

He had a point. Of course I knew what I was doing. I was a poet and I had to behave like one. It was what people expected. And it carried on throughout the Tour. I roared and drank my way around America and when I went back to Britain I had almost no money to show for the three months. Cat was furious, as she had every right to be.

"You're a waster, Dylan. Three months of getting pissed every night and there's no money to pay the bills. Or your income tax."

What it meant, of course, was that on the next trip to the States, Caitlin insisted on coming with me. And that was an utter disaster. It wasn't just one person spending money and drinking like a fish, now there were two of us. Cat made the most of her chance – and she managed to offend as many people as I had done on that first trip.

I didn't want to go back to America, not after that. But writing poetry was becoming harder and harder. Sometimes I went months without writing more than a few lines. I was working on *Milk Wood* but even that, doggerel as it was, took so much time and effort. There were days when I really thought it was all gone, forever.

So in the end I agreed to go back. Twice more, I went, both times without Cat. She hated it, screamed and swore at me, threatened to leave me.

"I know what you'll be doing!" she yelled. "You'll be drinking and getting off with women in every college in the country."

"Oh come on, Cat," I countered. "I'll be reading poems, that's all."

"You'll be drunk the whole damned time. You can't control yourself."

"Oh Cat, you know how I miss you when I'm out there."

She snarled. "Do I? I know you write me stupid love letters all the time, sickly things that belong on the fire. My stomach turns every time the postman comes down the path. You write the letters and send them but don't think I believe them. I know how easily lying comes to you."

"Not in this case, Cat. I love you, I don't want to go. But I have to. Cat, Cat, I promise I'll behave myself. And I'll bring back lots and lots of lovely American dollars. We'll be rich."

She wouldn't have any of it. She knew what was waiting for me, knew I couldn't resist any temptation that came my way. She knew it

75

would kill me, all that drinking and running around the country. She knew I couldn't cope with being the famous poet or with people being so kind to me.

By the time of my last visit I was having blackouts and there were days I could hardly breathe. I'd put on a lot of weight – the skinny little poet of the 1930s had gone forever. I should have known going to America again was bad for my health, maybe even fatal. But it was money and, if I care to think about it, I was running again, running away from all the responsibilities and problems in my life. America was a great bolt hole.

And then, in December 1952, my father died. It had been coming for months and at the end he was in such pain that I sat there and willed him to die. To ease his suffering. A far cry from the one poem I wrote about his end – 'Do Not Go Gentle Into That Good Night' – which really begged him to stay and fight. It was selfish, that poem, but I had never realised how much I needed him, not until it was too late. It's a hell of a thing to wish your father would die. I know it was for his sake but I don't think I've ever forgiven myself.

My mother was upbeat about his death,

dealing with it as usual with platitudes and Welsh words of wisdom.

"He's happy now," she said. "No more suffering, no more pain."

"How can you say that?" I asked.

She shrugged. "Because it's true, Dylan. Did you want to see him carry on in pain like that? I think you loved him too much for that."

She had a point. Wherever Dad was – and I still don't know if I believe in Heaven – he was finished with suffering now. So although I was sad, desperately sad, in a way I was also happy for him. So many mixed emotions were going round in my head.

Sometimes I would sit in my writing shed, that lonely crow's nest above the water, and think about things. I was supposed to be writing but I couldn't do it. My inspiration was gone and I couldn't work out why – until I realised that my father stood for the past. The past that was so important to me. And now that was gone and I was finished as a writer.

It is now mid-morning and Brinnin and Liz Reitell have not returned to Dylan's hospital room. Good luck to them, John Berryman thinks, they need a break, an hour or two away from this place; waiting here would drive anyone crazy. And so he sits on peacefully, staring at the silent poet and trying hard to work out how all this happened.

Nurses come and go, sweeping into the room like sailing ships and then leaving, most of them without saying a word. One, however, hovers by the door.

"I'll have to come back to give him a bath in a little while," she says. "We have to do it every couple of days – stops him getting bed sores. I'll be back soon, say in an hour. Are you all right here till then?"

Berryman nods. "No problem. Say, do you know where my friends are?"

"In the restaurant," she says, indicating with her arm. "They must be on their tenth cup of coffee by now. Do you want me to fetch them?"

"No," he says, shaking his head. "Let them have a break. They've been keeping him company here for days on end. They deserve a little time off."

The nurse eases out and Berryman continues his watch.

Almost there. I feel so tired. I think I've said it all, said all I want to say. Nearly, anyway. It's time to stop worrying and fretting, time to stop thinking.

In the years to come I'm sure they'll all wonder what killed me. Was it the drugs my doctor gave me? Was it the alcohol? Or my lifestyle? Was it diabetes or asthma? I can imagine the debates they're going to have. The truth is I just don't want to go on any more. I've reached the end, I have nothing more to say.

OK, I am supposed to be writing a libretto for Stravinsky. They've been talking about it for years but a few weeks ago the deal was finally done. Big money beckons. So what? I've earned big money before – and spent it quickly enough.

No, truth to tell, I don't have the words any more. And for someone who has always ever had just one aim, to write books and poems and stories, that's a frightening prospect. Frankly, I don't know if I can do it any more. The way the writing is going now, it would take me ten years to write that libretto and I don't think Stravinsky can wait that long!

Writing is automatic, you sit at your desk

and do it. What's important is the thing that makes you want to write, the motivation. And I've got nothing left to write about. Everything is going, or has already gone. Everything I ever cared about, anyway.

Swansea, my Swansea, flattened by bombs, and all the well-known places wiped out. Swansea meant so much to me. Even if I do criticise it and call it names, I don't mean any of them. Lying again, this time to myself. I remember talking once on a radio programme, saying something supposedly witty like "Swansea bore me, now I'm boring Swansea". See, even now, at this late stage, I can't stop telling stories. I just hope I didn't bore anyone, whether they're from Swansea or not.

Then my father, that sad and proud old man. His death seems to have drawn a line under the past, cut me off from that real or imagined world of childhood and adolescence. I think, when I care to look at it, everything I've ever done – all the poems, all the books, all the radio scripts – was for him. I wanted to make him proud of me. And he was, in the end, very proud.

Last but certainly not least, there's Caitlin. I've lost her. It was my own fault, I know that, but it doesn't make it any easier to take. She was unfaithful, many times, just like me. But as she often said, her affairs didn't matter, they were just tiny moments, things that didn't mean anything. With me, she said, it was different. With me there was a brain involved.

I wonder if it's possible to love two or even three women at the same time? There was a woman I met during my first American tour. I think I loved her for a while. She came over to Britain and we met up in London. It didn't work out but Cat got to know about it and threatened to end our marriage. We worked through it, I think. And now there's Liz. None of it, not that first American woman or Liz, means I love Cat any less. If anything I think I love her more.

It all confuses the hell out of me, I can tell you. I'm a simple soul – all I ever wanted to do was write poems and get paid for it. Not too much wrong with that, is there? The trouble is the world isn't made that way.

So many problems. I just want peace and one thing is clear – there's no peace in this world. Maybe in the next. That's if there is a next world. I don't care any more. Everything's finished, written out. I'm too tired to worry any more. Time to call it a day.

It's been a good innings. Listen to that, a cricket image, right at the end. My friend John Arlott, the cricket reporter and broadcaster, would be pleased. There have been bad times and lately the bad have counted for more than the good. But in the main I've done what I wanted. I wrote poems, perhaps half a dozen great ones that will last and be read in a hundred years. We'll see. I can't think any more, I'm too tired.

That's it, game over. Time to go.

The nurse appears in the doorway, her arms full of soap, blankets and bottles. She smiles at Berryman and wrinkles her nose.

"Time for his bath," she says. "Are you stopping? You can give me a hand, if you like."

Berryman shakes his head and holds up his hands.

"Not me. A private time between him and his nurse." He stands and moves to the doorway. "I'll just step outside for a cigarette. Let me know when you've finished."

He goes out. Standing in the corridor he takes out a crushed packet of Stuyvesant, opens it and places a cigarette in his mouth. He strikes a match but before he has time to light the cigarette he hears a call from the hospital room.

"Mr Berryman, come quickly."

He rushes back into the room. The nurse is standing beside the bed, the oxygen tent pushed back. Dylan is lying on his right side, mouth open and not breathing.

"It happened just as I turned him onto his side," says the nurse. "He just gave a big sigh and died. Simple and as calm as that."

"Are you sure? Sure he's really dead?"

"I'm sure."

"And there's nothing you can do?"

The nurse shakes her head.

"I'd better tell the others," Berryman says and turns, once more, out of the door.

He pauses for a moment, drawing in breath through his nose. Then, for some strange reason, he begins to run along the corridor towards the restaurant. He runs, even though he knows that speed will not help Dylan now. He meets John Brinnin and Liz at the door to the café.

"Where were you?" he gasps. "He's gone."

"Gone," says Brinnin, "what do you mean, gone?"

"Dead, he's dead. Just now as the nurse was getting ready to bathe him. He's dead, John, dead."

John Brinnin pushes through the crowd that has gathered behind him and takes Liz Reitell's hands in his. Together they go slowly towards Dylan's room.

In the room nurses are already dismantling the oxygen tent. After a while they leave Liz and Brinnin alone with Dylan's body. The poet's eyes are shut and he seems, finally, to be at peace. Brinnin puts his hands around Dylan's feet. They are ice cold, all the warmth having fled the body. Liz lightly kisses Dylan's forehead.

Then they stand at the foot of the bed, each of them lost in their own thoughts. They do not cry, there is no place for tears, and there is no sound in the white room.

Quick Reads

Books in the Quick Reads series

Quick Reads 📖

Fall in love with reading

Headhunter
Jade Jones

Accent Press

Petite North Walian Jade Jones certainly lived up to her nickname at London 2012 when she fought her way to become Britain's youngest Olympic Champion. Using her trademark style of scoring extra points by targeting kicks to her opponent's head, Jade secured her place in Olympic history as Britain's most successful taekwondo player adding the Olympic Gold to her medal collection.

In *Headhunter* Jade, still only 20, describes how her passion for the sport was sparked at the age of eight when her Grandad first took her to a class at his local club. Over the years her ambition and hard work has paid off, winning her numerous Sportswoman of the Year awards. As she works towards her Olympic goals for Rio 2016, Jade follows her mantra 'If you believe … you can do it! Try hard enough and you can!'

Quick Reads 📖

Fall in love with reading

Lionheart
Richard Hibbard

Accent Press

When Lions and Wales rugby star Richard Hibbard crashed into George Smith under a clear night sky in Australia, it felt as though the tremors might have rocked Sydney Harbour Bridge.

Smith was the 'Mr Indestructible' of Australian rugby, yet he was helped off the pitch. Hooker Hibbard simply shook his trademark blond locks and carried on helping the Lions earn their 2013 series victory. Soon, pictures of "Hibbz" celebrating in the dressing room with James Bond actor Daniel Craig were being beamed around the world.

In *Lionheart*, the Ospreys star reflects on his long and often rocky road to the top of world rugby: from his roots in Port Talbot, to his stint with rugby league club Aberavon Fighting Irish, to himself fighting back from countless serious injuries.

About the Author

Phil Carradice is a novelist, poet and historian. He has written over 40 books, including *Snapshots of Welsh History – Without the Boring Bits*. He also broadcasts regularly on BBC Radio 3 and 4 and presents the BBC Wales radio programme *The Past Master*. He writes a weekly blog for BBC Wales History and regularly appears on television programmes like *The One Show*